I0586966

The Dark Lord's Risk Assessor

Nikki Moyes

Moyes Publishing

Contents

A New Client

Janet Higgins breezed into the office of Duffleooffer & Co Risk Assessors bright and early on Monday morning. She headed straight to her desk in the corner away from the distraction of windows. After all, windows weren't a necessity when work required inspections outdoors and Janet was always first to volunteer for even the most difficult assignments.

She glanced briefly at the framed letter hung on the wall of her cubicle. From a client and addressed to her boss, the letter referred to Janet as 'a fully qualified psychopath'. She'd been pleased the client had recognized she was fully qualified and kept the letter as a fond reminder.

Janet set her handbag on the desk, turned on the computer and headed to the kitchen to make a cup of tea. On the way, she nodded to the hallway portrait of

Albert P. Duffleooffer, the founder of the company and the holder of the record for most deficiencies issued to a client on a single assignment. No other risk assessor in the country had ever matched his total, although Janet held grand aspirations to match Mr Duffleooffer. Back at her desk, Janet scrolled through the company's open tasks while her co-workers filed in.

"Good morning. What a gorgeous day," she greeted them cheerfully. Her co-workers grunted and glanced suspiciously at the gloomy weather outside the window.

The majority of Janet's co-workers were not only terrible morning people, but also males. In fact, many clients were surprised to see a female risk assessor show up at their businesses, but as Janet explained it, her role was to tell men what they were doing wrong and give them a list of things to fix. Janet felt that females were uniquely suited to the role. She was so successful with her role that she'd never felt the need to find a husband. After all, what was the use of a husband other than someone for her to point out mistakes to and give to-do lists, and Janet got plenty of that at work. She was more than happy to come home at the end of a successful day to her two cats and no husband.

Janet looked over the week's tasks, but there was nothing particularly exciting or difficult. She had finally settled on a task that would likely require a Prohibition Notice, when her boss Mr Rickmore called her into his office. Janet grabbed her ever present notepad and pen, and took the seat opposite Mr Rickmore's desk.

"Good morning, Mr Rickmore. Did you have a great weekend?" Janet beamed at him.

"Humph." He looked her up and down to see she was already dressed for assignment in her durable work trousers, high-vis shirt and steel-capped boots. "I've received an unusual request by a potential new client. The job will likely be difficult, with many obstacles."

"That sounds excellent. Where is it and are they ready to start today?" Janet hovered her pen over the notepad.

"The person who contacted me is the new advisor to the Dark Lord of the Mortiferous Mountains in the east of Fantasyland." He paused to let that sink in.

"I do enjoy a good mountain hike," Janet replied cheerily.

"Apparently the last five advisors all died of unexpected and gruesome deaths."

"Nothing is unexpected if a proper risk assessment has been completed," Janet said. 'One fatality is one too many. This sounds like an emergency. I'll pack immediately."

Mr Rickmore passed over a pack of information, including directions and an overview of the issues as reported by the new advisor.

"Be careful. This operator could be very dangerous."

"I'm always careful, Mr Rickmore." Janet took the package and headed back to her desk.

She pulled out her inspection backpack and made sure it was sufficiently stocked with spare work clothes, deficiency lists, Prohibition and Improvement Notices, pens, laptop, torch, tape measure, one of those little hammers used to tap on things, and an assortment of other implements she had found useful over the years.

By the time Janet had checked she had everything she might need for an extended initial consultation of a high-risk operator, the administration officer appeared with travel arrangements. Janet accepted the documents from Miranda, said a hearty goodbye to her co-workers which was mostly ignored, shouldered her backpack and left to catch the train to Fantasyland.

The train journey was uneventful, the transport company having been audited by Duffleoooffer & Co Risk Assessors on a previous occasion. Janet passed the journey by going over the notes provided by the Dark Lord's new advisor. The organisation had the worst record she had even seen, with regular injuries and fatalities.

Once at the border of Fantasyland, Janet found a cart driver to take her up to the Mortiferous Mountains for a rather excessive fee, but there appeared to be no other cart available due to them all breaking down the moment she arrived. Clearly their maintenance was not up to standard.

The driver dropped her halfway up the winding mountain track, within sight of a narrow bridge spanning a fast-flowing creek, before he hurriedly turned his horses around and whipped them into a gallop back in the direction they had come.

Janet glanced up at the towering mountain range still above her. Trees gave way to tenacious shrubs clinging to cliff faces. Sharp, craggy peaks jutted out at various angles before disappearing under a bank of dense clouds. The stonework of what she assumed was the Dark Lord's castle peeked out through a gap in the mountains. Glimpses of the track wound its way upwards to Janet's destination.

What a magnificent location for a rock climbing holiday.

Janet slipped her notepad and pen into her pocket before carefully assessing the bridge before her. No handrails, no raised edge, no edge markings. She walked to the edge of the track to peer at the side of the ridge. Massive timber logs created the underside of the bridge, although by the mossy growth, it had been in place for many years without regular maintenance.

Her gaze dropped to the flowing creek. On the far bank, a twisted human body lay half submerged in water. Janet quickly scanned her surroundings, but she was alone. Out came the binoculars from a side pocket of her bag. She focused on the body. It was fresh. The throat had been ripped out and the chest was still. The man's uniform matched the emblem on the packet Janet had received about the Dark Lord. As he was obviously deceased, Janet made a quick note of her initial observations so she could notify his employer to retrieve his body and start an investigation.

She returned her attention back to the bridge, stomping one foot carefully on the deck. The timbers reverberated with a reassuring solid sound. With no better access to the castle, she'd need to cross.

Janet pulled a metal spike, hammer, and coil of rope from her bag. After securing the spike firmly in the ground, she attached a safety line to the spike and then her waist. She shouldered her backpack but kept the hammer in hand. The man hadn't appeared to have died from a fall.

As she reached the middle of the bridge, a moss-covered troll leapt out from under the timber deck and landed heavily on the bridge with a bellow. Janet froze, waiting to see if the structural integrity of the bridge was sufficient to support one woman with a full backpack and an exuberant troll. The timbers groaned briefly but held.

"I don't think it's wise for both of us to remain on this bridge. There is no maximum allowable load limit posted," Janet pointed out.

"You must answer a riddle before you may cross into the Dark Lord's domain." The troll roared, flashing two rows of sharp, filthy teeth.

"I've been invited here to conduct a risk assessment on the Dark Lord's operation." Janet balanced carefully on the bridge as she reached into her backpack for her risk assessor's laminated letter of introduction. She waved it at the troll. "Under Section 17 of the Risk Assessors' Act of 1538, it is an offense to impede me from carrying out my duties as a risk assessor."

"People in poverty have this. If you eat this, you will die. What is it?" The troll ignored Janet's speech in order to deliver its riddle.

"I've got nothing," Janet replied. "Wouldn't you be better off asking my name, purpose of visit, and if I have an appointment, instead of riddles?"

The troll roared loudly and leapt off the bridge into the water below.

"That was rather rude, not to mention dangerous," Janet muttered as she made her way carefully to the other side of the bridge.

Once safely on firm ground, she secured the safety line to a tree trunk beside the bridge for use upon her return, put away her letter of introduction, and made a quick note about unsuitable bridges and appropriate questions to ask visitors. That done, she took a sip of water from the pouch in her bag and started the hike up towards the castle.

It had been a long while since Janet had been able to take such a satisfying hike during work hours and she was almost sad when the drawbridge of the Dark Lord's castle came into view hours later, but there were deficiencies to be issued and Janet enjoyed that almost as much.

As she approached the drawbridge covering a moat, four guards carrying a mix of swords and maces charged out of the castle grounds where they had been loitering in heavy armour. Dark visors obscured their faces under their helmets. Janet stopped, whipped out her pen and flipped to a fresh page in her notepad.

"What training have you been provided with those weapons?" she asked.

The guards skidded to a halt, facing her general direction, although it was difficult to tell if they could see her sufficiently through the opaque visors. The one in the middle of the group spoke up. "Training?"

"Yes, training. Who keeps the records of which guards have been trained in each weapon?"

The guards glanced at each other. "We just pick the one we like the look of," the one with two missing fingers said.

Janet's eyes gleamed. She dropped her backpack on the ground and pulled out her Prohibition Notice pad.

"Do not use weapons," Janet muttered to herself as she filled out her first form. "Reason: no training presents a risk to the safety of persons."

Janet signed the form, ripped the top copy off the pad and taped it to the chest of the nearest guard. He lifted his visor to see what was stuck to his armour.

A scrawny, frazzled man in a rumpled flowing purple cloak and crumpled velvet pointed hat dashed out of the castle grounds as Janet stepped past the confused guards.

"Wait! Stop! Don't attack!" he yelled as he ran forward.

Janet waited for him to reach her before she thrust out a hand. "Janet Higgins of Duffleooffer & Co Risk Assessors. You must be the Dark Lord's advisor."

The slender man doubled over trying to catch his breath while he stared at her outstretched hand in puzzlement, before straightening and offering a limp hand. A frown crossed Janet's brow, however there was no legislation that prevented substandard handshakes, so she was unable to list the interaction as a deficiency.

"Ah, yes, Advisor to the Dark Lord, that's me. Richard Tumberridge" the man offered, before glancing past her. "Apologies for the rough reception. I wasn't expecting someone so quickly. Where is the risk assessor?"

"That would be me. Considering the state of your operation, my manager Mr Rickmore thought it prudent to send the best." Janet raised one eyebrow and proceeded to stare the man down until he felt suitably cowed over his question.

"Oh." He shuffled from foot to foot. "Where's the man I sent to wait by the troll's bridge?"

"Mr Tumberridge, I regret to inform you that I encountered a deceased male dressed in the Dark Lord's colours beside the bridge. Once you have safely retrieved the body, I expect you to provide me with a full report of your investigation into his death, including future preventative actions, before I leave."

The man swallowed nervously. "Of course, Ms Higgins. Shall we, ah, proceed inside? I'll give you a quick rundown of the operation and show you to your quarters for your stay. Mr Rickmore said this could take some time."

"I familiarised myself with the information you provided on the way here. If you don't mind, I'll make notes on my way to my room. Firstly, your guards are prohibited from using weapons until they are fully trained. Secondly, do they normally stand out in the weather dressed in armour without appropriate protection?"

"Ummmm," Mr Tumberridge said.

Janet made a quick note in her book - *'protection from weather'* before she walked up to the moat.

"Don't get too close. The crocodiles get hungry."

"Hmmmmm." Janet scribbled *'moat - no railing, risk of fall/drowning/being eaten, captive animals not sufficiently fed (animal welfare issue?), no access to get out of water once in'*. Mr Tumberridge peered over her shoulder as she wrote.

"You're going to need a temporary barrier and warning signs around this moat until you have a permanent arrangement," Janet waved a hand at the unsafe area.

"But it's designed to keep people out. What if a hero comes along and tries to attack the castle?"

"How many of your own guards have slipped into the moat?"

"Only one this year. I've been told we haven't lost many since the last big battle with the hero a generation ago. The hero's son is probably of age soon, hence my request to Duffleooffer & Co Risk Assessors. People in my position tend to have short lifespans, but I recently married and my wife insisted it was a prestigious role with good pay. It even comes with a widow allowance in case of my untimely death, although I'd prefer it didn't come to that."

"One workplace fatality is one too many. If you follow all my directions in improving the organisation, your wife won't be needing a widow allowance. Now this drawbridge has no railings either. If someone was to cross in poor lighting or when the timbers are wet, they could slip and fall in the water. Again, I'm going to need a temporary barrier in place, preferably by morning."

Janet retrieved her backpack from where she had left it on the ground and crossed down the centre of the drawbridge with the harried man following close on her heels. Once inside the castle grounds, Mr Tumberridge attempted to take the lead.

"Your room is this way, Ms Higgins."

Janet paused to make a few more notes - *'no protection from the weather, nearest drinking water, heating, lighting after dark?'* before following the advisor.

Mr Tumberridge led her through a maze of gloomy, narrow corridors inside the castle, before finally stopping at a heavy timber and steel door. "Here is your room for the evening. Dinner will be served in one hour. To find the dining hall, head down this corridor to the end, make a right, then halfway along take another right and then the next left."

Janet glanced down the corridor in both directions. "Where is the nearest exit? There are no exits marked. Nor have I seen any firefighting equipment since we entered the castle."

"We can't have exits marked. If a hero broke in, he'd know how to get out again."

"And if your hero happened to start a fire while he was in the castle, it would result in numerous fatalities. Now if you can just tell me where the nearest exit is and emergency muster point?"

"Opposite direction to the dining hall to get out. Take the first left, then second right, follow to the end and take a right and another left. But no one has mentioned there being a muster point," Mr Tumberridge said.

"Hmmm," Janet said as Mr Tumberridge backed away hurriedly.

Janet opened a side pocket of her backpack, pulled out a packet of glow-in-the-dark arrow stickers, and followed the directions provided, marking the exit route with the stickers as she went. Once the exit had been located, she headed back to her room, pulled out her spare fire extinguisher which she placed in an easy to access location by the door. With twenty minutes to spare, Janet freshened up in the attached bathroom then headed off to the dining hall.

The din in the dining hall dimmed as Janet walked in after finding her way through the maze of corridors. The space was half filled with a variety of people who all turned to stare at her. A range of smells, some pleasant, some not so much, wafted in from an open doorway. Janet ignored the dining hall and barged through the open kitchen doors.

Steam rose from multiple saucepans. A pan caught fire, flames reaching towards the greasy ceiling. Janet whipped out her ever-present notepad and pen.

"You can't be in here." A kitchen hand rushed forward to shoo Janet out of the room.

"I am the risk assessor. I will go wherever I need to go to do my role. Where is your fire management plan?"

A dozen people scurried back and forth, stepping over a spill of some sort, while the kitchen hand stood there trying to remember how to form words. A harried chef momentarily forgot about the spill and skidded into a bench. The tray he was holding clattered to the floor along with several dozen pastries. He bent down to return the dropped food to the tray before shoving it in the direction of the serving window.

Advisor Tumberridge dashed through the doorway and halted in front of Janet. "Is there something I can assist with? Perhaps you'd like to take a seat in the dining hall? The food will be out shortly."

"There is too much work to be done. Kitchens are a high fire risk. The door is open and not fire rated. I can see no fire extinguishers or fire blankets. The pan is on fire." Janet made her way around the kitchen, weaving through startled kitchen staff and dropping a lid over the flaming pan, as she continued to rattle off her list. "Unguarded cutting blades, spill on the floor," she paused to move a small step ladder over the offending patch, "lack of food hygiene, serving food that has been on the ground, raw chicken being prepared on the same chopping boards as the vegetables, open fireplace with no heat protection, full cauldrons exceed manual handling limits. What safety training do the staff undergo?"

"Training?" Mr Tumberridge wrung his hands together.

"Never mind. I'll write you up a deficiency list. This kitchen is not suitable for the preparation of food. It will need to be shut down. I hope you have cold rations available. Clean up the spill and make sure that fire is out. I'm heading back to my room to start my report. I'll see you bright and early in the morning to meet the Dark Lord."

Janet swept out of the room and weaved her way through the corridors. Back at her room, she pulled a protein bar from her bag and munched on it as she wrote up another Prohibition Notice.

The Dark Lord's Project

—◦✦◦—

T imid tapping sounded on Janet's door moments before she was about to set off to find the advisor.

"Good morning, Mr Tumberridge ," Janet chirped as she strode out of the room with her backpack.

"Is it?" He glanced around, but as they were inside with no windows, there was no way to verify Janet's word regarding the state of the morning.

"It's always a great morning," Janet replied as she followed the advisor through a maze of corridors and up and down countless flights of stairs.

After about fifteen minutes, they arrived at a heavy, dark timber door. Mr Tumberridge pounded the flat of his palm on the surface before turning the handle and shouldering the door open. Janet followed him into the dimly lit room.

"Dark Lord, sir?" Mr Tumberridge called out. "I have the risk assessor here to see you."

Janet glanced around the room. *Insufficient lighting. Various unidentified objects on the floor creating trip hazards. Sharp corners on the furniture she could barely make out in the gloom. Still no marked exits or fire control equipment.* Janet made a few quick notes in her booklet.

A tall, lanky man swept across the room towards them, his black cape flapping around him as he approached. His face was obscured under the hood of the cape.

Janet thrust out a hand. "Janet Higgins, senior inspector at Duffleooffer & Co Risk Assessors."

The Dark Lord stared at her hand for a moment before grasping it firmly. "Lord Vern Flufflebutte."

He dropped her hand and turned to address his advisor. "Dick, I told you worrying was unnecessary. No one has died since Tuesday."

"No fatalities in a week? That's hardly something to be proud of. Not to mention untrue. The man sent to meet me was killed in what may have been a troll attack," Janet said firmly.

"That is outside castle grounds-" the Dark Lord growled.

"Ah! No excuses. Mr Tumberridge provided me with an overview of your organisation. You have a terrible track record. It's surprising you still have anyone working for you. But we can fix this. What is the purpose of your business? What are you trying to achieve?"

"Destruction," Lord Flufflebutte narrowed his eyes beneath his hood and paused for a moment before adding, "and fear."

"Well, you've certainly got the fear aspect under control. All your employees are afraid of dying while working for you. Bringing about destruction is no excuse for having an unsafe workplace."

Lord Flufflebutte crossed his arms and glared at Janet. "It's how my father and grandfather ran the castle," he snapped.

"We're not living in the dark ages anymore, Lord Flufflebutte. It's not acceptable for employees to die at work. And regularly training new staff can be costly. Retention is a much better choice. I've been making a list of deficiencies for you to rectify before you continue operations."

"But I have a fair princess to kidnap!" Lord Flufflebutte exclaimed.

"Any dastardly business will have to wait until you can provide a safe workplace for your employees. Let's walk through this kidnapping project. I assume you haven't completed a risk assessment yet?" Janet asked.

"No..." Mr Tumberridge answered when Lord Flufflebutte continued glaring at her.

Janet turned to the advisor and waited for him to continue.

"The Dark Lord has no successor. He needs a wife, and the local kingdom has four unwed princesses."

Lord Flufflebutte interrupted, "The plan is to storm the kingdom, capture one of the princesses and return here. Then we will arrange for an elaborate ceremony to be held one month later as per Flufflebutte custom."

"Hmmmm." Janet scribbled notes.

"During that time, we expect a hero and his team to attack. We will capture them and lock them in the dungeon until after the wedding."

"Let's go back to the beginning." Janet tapped her pen on her notepad. "You've met the princesses? Which one is more likely to want to be your wife?"

Both men stared at her.

"The Dark Lord hasn't met any of the princesses." Mr Tumberridge eventually admitted.

"Forcing someone to marry you is a terrible idea. A princess who doesn't want to be here will be waiting to be rescued. She may even try to sabotage the castle, any projects you are working on, or trick your guards into releasing your prisoners. All hazardous activities. What you need is a woman who consents to be your wife."

"Consent?" Both men appeared confused.

"Yes, consent. A woman who is enthusiastic about becoming your wife instead of a begrudging 'only if you promise not to murder my family' kind of girl," Janet explained.

"How am I meant to find a wife if I don't kidnap one?" Lord Flufflebutte demanded.

"Have you considered a personal ad? There are plenty of women who go for the tall, dark and handsome look. I'm assuming you own your own castle and are running your own business? A business that will be successful if you follow my directions and fix the deficiencies I'll be issuing."

"So, a woman will want to marry the Dark Lord and live in the castle?" Mr Tumberridge asked, his brow still furrowed as his pointy hat threatened to slip over one eye.

"That's the idea. Think of this woman as a potential personal and business partner. You want to surround yourself with a team that will work towards common goals. A kidnapped princess will cause way more problems than it's worth."

"Dick, do as the little woman says." Lord Fluffle-butte gestured grandly towards Janet.

"Of course, Dark Lord, sir. Should we continue with the risk assessment first?" Mr Tumberridge glanced at Janet as though waiting to be rescued himself.

"Perhaps you should show me these dungeons," Janet said.

"This way." Lord Flufflebutte grabbed the edge of his cape to sweep dramatically out of the room.

Janet made another note in her book before stepping carefully over the shaft of a mace discarded on the floor and followed the Dark Lord back through the maze of corridors, none of which were marked with exits.

Growls echoed off the damp and slippery walls, as the three wound their way down into the depths of the castle. *Poor lighting, no handrails, no non-slip surfaces,* Janet paused to write. She pulled out her gas monitor, switched it on, and clipped it to the pocket of her shirt. Before putting her backpack on again, she pulled out her intrinsically safe headlamp to illuminate the tunnel.

A ginormous, toothy, scaled beast guarded the bottom of the staircase, attached only to a thick chain around its neck. The Dark Lord entered a two-digit code into a panel on the wall, causing a steel cage to drop down over the beast.

"The creature will destroy anyone who dares escape from my fortified dungeon," Lord Flufflebutte declared.

"Unless they have the two-digit code. Not very secure," Janet commented.

The Dark Lord scowled. Janet walked up to the cage to study the beast. It growled and lunged towards her. The chain around its neck cut through the scales, causing green blood to seep from the wound. Its breath momentarily set off the hydrogen sulphide alarm and Janet stepped back where the air was less toxic.

"What is it?" Janet asked.

"No idea. We call it Frank," Lord Flufflebutte replied.

"Well, Frank appears undomesticated and in urgent need of vetenary care. He's likely to become dangerous if left in his current condition."

"He's meant to be dangerous," Lord Flufflebutte bellowed, setting off an answering bellow from Frank.

"Dangerous to your enemies, or your employees?" Janet asked. "At the moment he appears more of a risk to your staff and if you don't attend to Frank's health,

I will be forced to report you to Animal Welfare. If that happens, they will likely look at rehoming Frank. You wouldn't want that now, would you?"

"No," Lord Flufflebutte replied sulkily before slinking past the cage and heading deeper into the dungeons.

"I suggest you hire an animal trainer once Frank's wounds have healed. Get him used to you and make sure he isn't aggressive around your employees. A beautiful animal like that needs to be treated with kindness and respect," Janet continued talking to the Dark Lord's hunched shoulders.

Janet looked back over her shoulder longingly, however she didn't think her cats would appreciate an additional housemate. "Also, extra forced ventilation wouldn't go astray. A bit of heavy breathing from Frank and everyone in his vicinity could be rendered unconscious."

As they travelled further into the tunnels, Mr Tumberridge slipped several times on the damp floor and had to be steadied by Janet whose boots had a sensible grippy tread. His squeak, as he lost his footing for the third time, alerted the two dungeon guards to their arrival. Both guards had dark visors covering their faces and a bunch of keys dangling from their belts.

"How many people have just walked into the dungeon?" Janet asked.

"Are you talking to us?" the taller guard asked.

"Yes. You are the ones on guard duty, aren't you?"

"Oh," he replied before peering carefully through his dark helmet. "There are two of you."

"I thought there were four," the other guard said.

"Is there a reason you're wearing helmets you can't see through?" Janet asked.

"It's part of the uniform."

"It makes them look intimidating," Lord Flufflebutte growled.

Both guards dropped into a bow. "Forgive us, my lord. We didn't see you there," they grovelled.

"My point exactly," Janet said. "They can't see what is happening in their work area. I suggest you either remove the dark visors, or if you must keep them, consider hiring vision-impaired staff who are accustomed to working in the dark. A few seeing-eye dogs would be both cute and practical."

"Fine," Lord Flufflebutte grumbled. "Dick, have the men remove their visors and then poke out their eyes."

"What!" Mr Tumberridge exclaimed.

"You will do no such thing." Janet stepped between the Dark Lord and the cowering guards. "You are not to blind these guards. There are hefty fines and jail time for employee injuries particularly involving reckless conduct."

Janet pulled out her Prohibition Notice and quickly scribbled a few directions, before handing it to the Dark Lord.

"You are prohibited from deliberately causing injury to your employees. Do you understand?" Janet asked.

"Yes," Lord Flufflebutte sulked.

"Now I'd like to see inside one of your cells. What are your names?" Janet asked the guards.

"I'm Aaron the Really Tall and this is Felix the Flippin' Stupid," the tall guard said as he pulled out his bunch of keys to search for the one that would open the nearest cell.

"I'm going to recommend that everyone undergo sensitivity training. Bullying and name calling should not be tolerated in a workplace."

"But that's what everyone calls him," Aaron the Really Tall said.

"Ah!" Janet held up a finger and Aaron pressed his lips together.

Everyone stood around uncomfortably counting the minutes until Guard Aaron finally managed to get the right key in the lock. He heaved the cell door open with a drawn-out creak. Janet deposited her backpack in the doorway so the door couldn't close behind her and stepped into the cell.

The cramped, windowless room was covered in a layer of slimy grime. What could have once been called a straw mattress lay against one wall. When Janet nudged it with her boot, two scrawny rats dashed out. A dirty, but thankfully empty bucket stood in the corner of the room. Three sets of ankle and wrist shackles dangled from the walls. A quick tap with the steel toe of her boot sent shards of rust scattering across the room.

"This is completely unsanitary, and those rusty chains and shackles are likely to give your prisoners tetanus. There are so many things wrong here. I'm just going to write you a list." Janet grabbed her bag and exited the cell.

She turned back to look at the guards who had now removed their dark visors but were keeping their distance from the Dark Lord just in case.

"What do you do if a prisoner falls ill while in the cell?" Janet asked.

"We immediately unlock the door and rush into the cell. One person assesses the casualty while the other monitors the remaining prisoners," Aaron said.

"How many prisoners are we talking about?" Janet asked.

"Everyone who came with the hero. A previous guard told us he once fitted ten in the same cell," Felix replied.

"Where is this guard now?"

"He retired. He was never quite the same after the head injury he got when the prisoners escaped. He said all he remembered was the hero choking, which would have ruined the planned execution, so they rushed in, and the guard woke up two days later," Aaron explained.

"Hmmm, that's what I was afraid of. We're going to have to work through a set of procedures for the dungeon. Perhaps have medical staff assigned down here when prisoners are being housed." Janet scribbled out another Prohibition Notice and taped it to the bars of the cell.

"You are prohibited from keeping prisoners until such time the cells are of a liveable standard and the guards aren't at risk. While we're at it, how about you find a better place to hang keys than just out of reach of the cell door?"

"Where are we meant to keep the spare keys?" Aaron asked.

"Pretty much anywhere else would be a huge improvement. I've seen enough here to issue the deficiencies. Lord Flufflebutte, I'd like to see your control room now, thank you."

The Dark Lord glowered at her for a long moment in which she stood her ground, before he once again grabbed the edge of his cloak and swept dramatically out of the dungeon. The effect was dampened when he nearly lost his footing in his non-safety shoes. The floor would definitely need a non-slip coating and maybe a rail. With a little bit of work, this area could become wheelchair accessible. Janet underlined her previous note and followed after the Dark Lord, with Mr Tumberridge trailing slowly behind.

Back up on what Janet assumed was the ground level, although without any windows, signage or marked exits it was difficult to tell, distant screams for help echoed off the walls. Janet pushed past Lord Flufflebutte and followed the desperate cries down another corridor to a heavy locked door. She rapped sharply on the wooden door.

"Yes, hello. Please let me out," a male voice yelled from the other side.

Janet turned to Lord Flufflebutte. "Unlock this door immediately."

"No, you don't need to see this section. The control room is down the other hall." The Dark Lord towered over Janet while he gripped the edge of his cloak like a puffed-up bird.

Janet took a step forward into his personal space and looked up at him. "I am here to assess your entire operation. You will unlock this door, or I will be forced to shut down your entire operation until improvements have been made."

The Dark Lord opened his cloak wider, but when Janet didn't flinch or break eye contact, he lowered his arms and slunk past her. He pulled out a key from underneath his cape, and slowly unlocked the door.

"Open it..." Janet encouraged.

With a huff, the Dark Lord swung the door open. The rumpled man on the other side took one look at the Dark Lord and scurried into the far corner of his prison. Janet slipped the key from the door so it couldn't be locked behind her and marched into the room.

Benches positioned haphazardly around the room, with sharp corners protruding into the walkways, were scattered with paper, test tubes, Bunsen burners and numerous devices of unknown usage in various stages of assembly. Janet's fingers twitched towards her Prohibition book.

"Locked doors are a fire hazard. If this room or the castle caught fire, this man would perish in the flames without any chance of escape," Janet admonished.

"I'd like to escape now, if that's alright with you," the man said.

"He can't leave. He hasn't finished my death ray," Lord Flufflebutte boomed from the doorway.

"This man doesn't want to be here. He's locked in a room that is a massive fire risk. There are so many things wrong here that I couldn't even begin to guess how this man might die," Janet said.

"I'd rather not die," the man spoke up. "I only went out for a loaf of bread and that was a month ago. My wife and baby have no idea what's happened to me. I was meant to clean the gutters. Missy is going to be really mad at me and the scary man hasn't even paid me."

Janet turned to Lord Flufflebutte. "What this man has described is a breach of working conditions. Having a death ray built by an unwilling scientist has the potential to be disastrous. You are prohibited from using this room in its current condition. This man needs to be paid for his time and to leave the premises."

"I can go right now." The man edged forward.

Janet narrowed her eyes at the Dark Lord still blocking the doorway. After a long moment, he stepped into the room and picked up an item off the bench as though that had always been his intention. "Dick, pay the man for his time," Lord Flufflebutte said over his shoulder.

The scientist shuffled past Janet to slip away. He paused in the doorway as Mr Tumberridge handed over a handful of crumpled notes from a pocket inside his cloak. "Does anyone know where I can pick up a loaf of bread?"

While Mr Tumberridge gave the scientist directions, Janet did a careful lap of the room making sure all power and gas was turned off, and all chemicals were correctly stored, before she stuck a prohibition notice to the door, ushered everyone out and locked the door. The key she tossed to the Dark Lord as the scientist scurried down the hall and out of sight.

"Now how am I going to get my death ray built?" Lord Flufflebutte whined.

"Don't be ridiculous," Janet replied. "Offer an impressively large grant and good living conditions and you'll have dozens of scientists applying for a position. Everyone knows a scientist can be attracted by enough money and resources for them to research their area of interest. Some will even science just to see if it can be done. There is absolutely no reason to kidnap an unwilling one. I'd like to see your control room now."

"This way, please." Mr Tumberridge held out an arm in the hopes that taking the lead may end the staring match between Ms Higgins and Dark Lord.

Janet gave a brief nod and followed after him, with Lord Flufflebutte looming behind them with another dramatic sweep of his cape. After several more twists and turns, the group reached the only marked door Janet had seen so far. The sign above the door read 'Not a Control Room - authorised personnel only - heroes keep out'.

"Hmmm." Janet made another note as Mr Tumberridge pushed open the door.

The three of them stepped into the room. Two rows of consoles on each side of the room were separated by a walkway down the middle. All screens faced the door, while all occupants faced away from the door. Janet stepped forward to read the nearest screen which happened to be a detailed layout of the castle including a list of the dungeon defences. The screen was at full brightness, probably so the operators could see them through the dark visors.

"Where is the security team?" Janet asked.

The nearest operator flinched so suddenly he almost fell from his chair, before looking blindly around the room for the voice. Several others jerked upright as though woken from sleep.

"Take those dark visors off," the Dark Lord boomed. "If I wanted you not to see, I'd hire blind guards."

Everyone in the room rushed to remove their helmets. "Sorry, my Lord," whimpered the one Janet had startled.

"I expect you all to be in proper uniform when I see you next," Lord Flufflebutte addressed the room above the heads of his employees.

"But...this is the uniform, my Lord, sir," a woman at the back of the room stuttered.

"How dare you question me." Mr Flufflebutte pulled out a laser gun and pointed it at the woman. Before he could fire off a round, Janet grabbed his arm and forced the weapon at the ground. The beam hit the floor, narrowly missing the Dark Lord's leather clad boots.

"Put that weapon away immediately," Janet demanded. "It is a violation of the Employee Rights Act to intentionally or negligently cause the death of a worker. Under Section 19.2, an employee has the right to seek clarification regarding directions. Do I make myself clear?"

Lord Flufflebutte glanced away from Janet's stare as he slipped the weapon away in his belt. "Yes," he mumbled.

"And? Your employee requires clarification," Janet prompted.

Lord Flufflebutte raised his chin and addressed the room, "as of half an hour ago, I decided to change the uniform. From now on you shall wear clear plexiglass visors, not dark ones. I can't have you all wandering around not able to see. Even if the dark ones do look classier."

"Who in here monitors castle security?" Janet wandered the room before stopping at a bank of camera feeds.

A man stood up, glanced quickly at the Dark Lord and back to Janet. "That would be me today."

"Did you see the three of us approach the control room door?" Janet asked.

"Ah, yes?" the man rubbed one eye before knocking a half empty coffee mug to the floor. He hurried to pick up the shattered pieces then rubbed the wet patch further into the carpet with one boot. Several other stains marked the floor around the desk.

"When was your last break?"

"Break?" Confusion crossed the man's face for a moment. "Oh, I haven't broken anything since my leg three months ago."

"Hmmm, and what time did you start your shift?" Janet clarified.

"Oh," the man peered blearily at a clock on one wall. "Twenty hours ago. Only four more to go."

Janet spun on her heel to face Lord Flufflebutte. "This man needs to be relieved of duty immediately, as should anyone else who has been working for at least twelve hours. From now on, all employees shall maintain appropriate work/rest hours."

"But we don't have enough minions!" Mr Tumberridge protested.

"I suggest you hire new employees and begin their training immediately." Janet narrowed her eyes at the man.

Mr Tumberridge wrung his hands and glanced quickly at the Dark Lord who was busy stalking around the room with an occasional sweep of his cape.

"Fine. Anyone who has worked longer than twelve hours, can go get some rest and be back here tomorrow," Mr Tumberridge announced before nearly being run down by the mass exit.

When Janet scanned the room, only three workers remained. They kept their heads down as though trying to go unnoticed.

"How many people are needed to run the control room?" Janet asked.

The Dark Lord swept the room with a glance. "Three will do."

"Actually, it takes fifteen to monitor all systems e-ffectively." The woman who spoke, slid down low in her chair when the boss glanced in her direction. Janet raised an eyebrow.

"I'll round up a new set of minions, before this woman shuts down my entire castle." Lord Flufflebutte stalked towards the door.

"While you're at in, have your IT team get in here and rearrange this equipment so that your employees are facing the door and can see anyone who enters. Screens containing secure information should not be able to be seen when people walk in the door," Janet said.

Lord Flufflebutte swept out of the room with a swish of his cape and muffled curses about 'whatever IT security was meant to be'.

The lights dimmed for a brief moment as the screens in the control flickered out simultaneously. The remaining workers slapped the sides of their monitors and wiggled cables until full power returned and all screens came back to life. Janet scanned the displays. The Dark Lord had vanished from the security monitors.

"Are any of you going to check the system?" Janet asked when no one moved from their work station.

"There's no need. The power has been doing that at least twice a day since I started. I've been told it's normal," Mr Tumberridge explained.

"Does the castle have surge protectors and when were the residual current devices last checked?" At the blank looks from the workers and advisor, Janet continued, "When was an electrician on site last?"

"Oh, if there's ever a problem, one of the guards goes looking for the loose wiring and twists any broken ends back together," one of the workers said.

"How many fatalities has this resulted in?" Janet asked.

"Not many, maybe a few a year not counting that one guy who was mauled to death by the rabid snow ferret that had been gnawing on the kitchen wiring."

"Hmmm." Janet quickly scribbled out a Direction Notice for a licensed electrician to conduct a compliance check on the whole castle.

"That sounds expensive," Mr Tumberridge examined the notice Janet handed him. "Are electrician's easy to kidnap?"

"There will be no kidnapping. You will hire the electrician, pay them for their work and fix all defects they find."

"The Dark Lord won't be happy," Mr Tumberridge.

"I won't be happy if you fail to comply with the Direction Notice," Janet replied.

Mr Tumberridge gulped. "I'll have someone sent to locate an electrician by the end of the day."

"Good, now what procedures do you have in place in case your security system is hacked?"

"If a hero was involved instead of a power outage, we'd hear the guards shooting."

"What if someone made it look like a power outage in order to get into the castle?" Janet asked.

Mr Tumberridge shrugged. "All of the important assets are heavily guarded and you've seen the dungeon's protection. No one can get in or out without an escort."

"Are there any children living at the castle?" Janet asked.

Mr Tumberridge blinked at her several times before answering. "The head housekeeper has a five-year-old child. There were several other children, but I haven't seen them in the last week."

"The five-year-old will do and a team of guards. We're going to conduct a drill."

The advisor fled the room with his brow furrowed, while Janet perused the room. She scribbled down various minor deficiencies in her notebook before coming across a big red button labelled 'self-destruct' situated in the middle of one console. The button had no safety cover and was positioned in a manner that a clumsy elbow could quite easily come to rest on.

"What exactly is this self-destruct button responsible for destroying?" Janet addressed those who remained in the room.

"The whole castle," a man said.

"How much evacuation time do you have once it's pressed?" Janet asked.

"I don't think there is time. You press it and the castle blows up along with any heroes and their friends who have breached our defences."

"And yourselves," Janet added.

"Well, yes...but the hero would be dead."

Janet sighed and dropped her bag on the floor. It had been a long time since she had encountered a workplace with such a complete lack of understanding around risk

prevention. She pulled out a roll of 'danger: do not en-
ter' tape and set about cordoning off the area surrounding the self-destruct button. As an added measure, she
hung a prohibition notice, forbidding the use of the
button, from the tape.

Mr Tumberridge reappeared with a child and ten
guards in tow. The advisor wrung his hands at Janet's
handiwork.

"I need a safety cover over the self-destruct switch
asap. Any explosive device must be disconnected until
a full review has been conducted on the system including preventative devices for accidental or reckless
activation, as well as a delay and alarm system to allow
employees sufficient time to evacuate."

"But what if that allowed a hero to escape?" Mr
Tumberridge protested.

"You can always plan what to do if that occurs, but if
everyone is dead and the castle destroyed, you not only
have no employees or place of business left, you will
have failed your General Safety Duties to those employees."

"Sir?" The captain of the guard addressed Mr Tumberridge, "I don't know what these General Safety Duties are, but the Dark Lord doesn't like failure. Do you
want me to disconnect the self-destruct?"

"Yes, go do that." Mr Tumberridge waved him away.

"Can I push the big button?" The five-year-old stared longingly at the off-limits button.

"I have something way more fun for you to do. I left a chocolate bar in one of the dungeon cells. If you can go fetch it without being seen by any of these guards, you get to eat it," Janet said.

The child's eyes widened. "Score!" He bolted from the room and Janet turned to address the others.

"Here is the scenario: the child is a hero who is trying to rescue his friend, the chocolate bar, from the dungeon. You know the hero is in the castle, you know where he is headed, you don't know where he is or if he has friends. Show me what you would do in this situation. I'm going to stay here and monitor from the control room." Janet glanced at her watch. "Any questions before you set off in search of the hero?"

One guard raised his hand and waited for Janet to acknowledge him before speaking. "Do you want the hero dead or alive?"

"Alive and unharmed," Janet replied. "Remember that he is a child and not an actual hero."

"Like a game." The guards nodded enthusiastically, gathered in a huddle to quickly discuss tactics, then filed out of the doorway, leaving Janet with the three workers and Mr Tumberridge.

Janet inspected the screen with the camera feeds. The child had already disappeared. The guards split into two groups to follow both directions of the corridor. At each intersection, they split again until each guard was on their own.

"Hmmm." Janet made a few notes. Mr Tumberridge crept closer to peer over her shoulder.

"They cover more ground if they split up," he said.

"If the enemy really was in the castle, they could easily pick off each guard before they could radio for help."

"Radio?"

"Please tell me that your guards are able to communicate with each other," Janet groaned.

"Most have exceptionally loud voices," Mr Tumberridge replied.

Janet covered her face with her hands and took a deep breath, before lowering her hands and addressing the advisor. "While the guards are wandering aimlessly around the castle in what I hope is the general direction of the dungeon because that's where I sent the child, I will assist you in writing procedures for your guards to follow."

She pulled out a large pad of paper from her backpack along with a collection of coloured pens. She
pointed Mr Tumberridge to a chair at a section of
bench not covered in unlabelled buttons. The next
hour passed with Janet throwing out terms like sit-
uational awareness, likelihood and consequence, and
communication procedures while Mr Tumberridge
scribbled notes on paper. Another page quickly filled
with items to be purchased such as hand-held radios
and ergonomic chairs. The door to the control room
swung open.

"Security system for the door. Keypad, scanner, or
similar." Janet pointed to the list for Mr Tumberridge
to jot down as the child, covered in grime and cobwebs,
walked up to her and held out a wrapper in a grubby
hand.

"It's empty," he said.

Janet reached into her bag and pulled out a wet wipe
to remove the chocolate and dirt smears from the child's
face. She brushed several cobwebs from his hair before
deciding his parents could deal with the rest of the mess.

"How did you get into the dungeon?" Mr Tumberridge exclaimed.

"The tunnels." The child pointed up.

"Air-conditioning ducts," Janet clarified at the advisor's confused look. "They're often wide enough to crawl through which can be a security risk in certain situations. I'd suggest you get in a heating and cooling technician to see how you can restrict access without impeding airflow."

"But what about the dungeon monster?" Mr Tumberridge exclaimed.

"I like Frank. He has scales." The child giggled.

"Did any of the guards see you?" Janet asked.

The boy shook his head and grinned.

"Excellent work, child. You may go back to your mother." Janet waved the boy away and he scampered from the room, nearly running into the Dark Lord on the way out.

A dozen men trailed in after him and set about turning the room around.

"Why are my guards loitering around the dungeon?" Lord Flufflebutte demanded.

"We were conducting a drill. The pretend hero just broke into your dungeon without being seen and escaped with his prize. So far no one appears to have noticed. Mr Tumberridge has pages of notes on how to improve next time. I think we are done with the control room for now. Let's discuss evacuation procedures in case of infiltration," Janet suggested.

"Oh, I have an excellent exit strategy." The Dark Lord swept out of the room with his cape billowing behind him.

Janet repacked her bag while Mr Tumberridge gathered his pile of papers before they followed the Dark Lord from the control room. They headed upwards this time, ascending damp staircases with no non-slip tread and a black mould problem, luckily Janet had a suitable mask on hand, before they emerged in the open, chilly air of the western castle turret.

The Dark Lord stood on the edge of the stone wall with his arms outstretched. Snowy mountains loomed behind and a light wind began to blow, ruffling the man's dark cloak in a dramatic and vaguely dangerous way.

"Lord Flufflebutte, you need to climb down from there before your cape tangles around your legs and you fall," Janet admonished.

"Nonsense, I've done this dozens of times. I just can't decide what my parting line should be as the hero rushes out of the stairway and sees me standing here."

"Excuse me?"

"I'm tossing up between 'I'll get you next time', 'this is just the beginning', or 'you have tiny hands'," Lord Flufflebutte continued.

"I'm not sure that's what you should be focused on right now," Janet replied.

"Of course it is. I need a famous last line before I do this." The Dark Lord took a step back and disappeared over the edge of the castle turret.

Mr Tumberridge let out a childish shriek while Janet dashed over to the wall and peered over the edge. A wide, stone slide wound its way down the side of the tower. Judging by the rough architecture, it had been there a long time. Various parts of the stone had been chipped away by years of weather. The Dark Lord was currently stuck halfway down the slide, facing head first, with one corner of his cape snagged on a section of jagged stonework.

Janet glanced over to Mr Tumberridge. "We'd better go check what's at the bottom of this slide before that cape tears," she paused, "and then I'm going to write up a very long deficiency list for you to action."

Janet gestured for the advisor to lead the way down the stairs. She followed with a grin on her face. She really had a chance to best Albert P. Duffleooffer's record-breaking list on this job. Lives were going to be saved whether they liked it or not.

Paperwork

"**Y**ou're back!" Assessor Scott Seymor exclaimed as Janet strode into office early-morning the following week.

It was unusual for anyone else to arrive first, and Janet eyed the space critically. Her heavy duty stapler, capable of stapling through a one-hundred-page report in a single go, sat on her colleague's desk. Scott stepped to the side, blocking her view of the pilfered stationary.

"I emailed Mr Rickmore about my need to stay on site for a few extra days. He should be expecting me today.

"Oh, right, of course." Scott sat on the edge of his desk and tried to subtly slide the stapler into a drawer.

"It took a while to explain the importance of having the right tool for the job instead of only hand-to-hand weapons and blow-up-the-planet weapons with nothing suitable for in-between tasks." Janet dropped her stack of paperwork beside her computer and conducted a quick inventory of her belongings.

"Then we got into the importance of fully reading instructions manuals before handling and using captured ancient artifacts." Janet rounded her desk, reached around Scott to snag her stapler, and returned to her pile of paperwork beside her computer.

"I explained material safety data sheets and proper storage of chemicals." She powered on her computer screen and waited for it to wake up.

"Then we discussed in length how he could improve his image with the local community and he eventually settled on funding an orphanage and setting up a trust for the families of his deceased employees. And I'm boring you..."

"Oh, no," Scott's head jerked up as though he'd been listening to the whole spiel. "We were just concerned that you might have had...issues. The Dark Lord has a reputation for killing people who...upset him, and you have a tendency to be..." he trailed off with a vague wave of one hand.

"Really? I had no issues with him, apart from being sulky. Now there's a man who's not used to being told no. I can tell you and the others all about it over some celebratory cupcakes after work today."

"What are we meant to be celebrating?"

Janet's face broke into a huge grin as she reached for her deficiency book. She held it up and flipped through the pages. She would have preferred to have one of those movie-style scrolls that unrolled in an impressive length across the floor, but she had been unable to find something appropriate at her local stationary store.

"Five more deficiencies issued than Albert P. Duffleooffer's record breaking total. That would make me the new record holder and that is worth celebrating."

"Right, well I'd better just go..." Scott's face took on a pained expression as he pointed a thumb over his shoulder, then walked out of the office despite there being a good eight hours before knock-off time.

Janet shook her head over his unsatisfactory work ethic and settled in at her desk to finalise her paperwork so she could move on to her next challenge.

***

Four months later:

"A letter has arrived for you, Janet." Miranda handed over the envelope then loitered while Janet opened it.

"It's from Mr Tumberridge, the Dark Lord's advisor." Janet scanned the contents of the letter.

"I thought you were finished with that job," Miranda replied.

"They've rectified most issues, but there are still a couple of outstanding items I've been working with them on."

Miranda sidled away before Janet could go into detail.

Dear Ms Higgins,

It's been fifty-four days without a death and twenty-three days without what you would call a "reportable incident". I've included proof that we've fixed the last couple of problems and the updated risk assessment and procedures you requested.

Work has been going well. New staff have been much easier to find since we started the community engagement projects. We've been keeping training records for all employees as you requested (attached). Quite a few of the orphans are keen to start work at the castle as soon as they are old enough.

The Dark Lord is back from his honeymoon and his new wife has taken an interest in the running of the castle. Lady Serena has been a great help with all this safety management stuff you've asked for and she can strike terror into anyone who doesn't follow procedures. She really is an excellent match for his Lord and I wanted to thank you for the advice around wording the personal ad.

As for my own wife, she doesn't seem overly happy that I've outlived the average employment period for an advisor in the castle. I've tried to talk to her, but she just mutters about life insurance and refuses to talk to me.

We've heard a rumour that a new hero is planning an attack, so I must go sit down with Lady Serena to review the risks and procedures around a possible assault.

Thank you for your time. I (and many others who work here) owe you my life.

Sincerely,

Richard Tumberridge.

A smile crossed Janet's face as she pinned the advisor's letter between the 'fully-qualified psychopath' letter and the wedding invitation to the Dark Lord's wedding. She hadn't attended, of course. It could have been perceived as a conflict of interest, but it had warmed her heart to receive an invitation.

Epilogue

One month later:

Janet returned to her desk after receiving a new assignment from Mr Rickmore to find a newspaper lying open on page three. Her co-workers, who had been whispering among themselves at Scott's desk, suddenly went silent and slunk away to their own areas. Several of them leaned around partitions as Janet picked up the newspaper and read the headline.

"Hero" Captured and Executed

Last week's attack by the so-called Hero, Aidaren and his rag-tag band of misfits on Fantasyland's Dark Lord has ended in disaster for the group. A close source to the hero said the misguided boy was avenging his father's lost hand. The father, of dubious character, attempted an assault on the Dark Lord a generation ago.

Due to Dark Lord Flufflebutte's recent charity work in the surrounding villages, the hero lacked the usual band of avenging orphans and was left unprepared for the upgraded defences of the Dark Castle.

The hero was captured and executed without the traditional time period that in the past allowed for further attacks and a rescue.

Castle spokesperson, Lady Serene Flufflebutte, told Fantasyland News that she was proud of her husband and the way the attack was thwarted with zero fatalities among castle employees. She reported that all injuries had been minor and treated immediately by the new in-house medical team.

The Flufflebuttes would like to thank the villagers for their support during this campaign and hope to be considered for this year's Employer of the Year Award.

No word yet from the hero's family and whether they will mount any further attacks in the face of overwhelming local support for the Dark Lord and his family.

"Zero deaths, well done." Janet reread the article again before pinning it to her wall. Another successful assignment. It was making an impact like this that really drove Janet to be the best risk assessor she could possibly be.

About the Author

Nikki Moyes was born in Victoria and has moved around Australia amassing an eclectic range of occupations including tall- ship watch leader, apiarist, rose farm hand, and sandwich artist. In her spare time she learns tissu, static trapeze, and aerial hoop (she couldn't decide on one) in case she needs to run off and join the circus.

You can find her here:

www.facebook.com/moyes.nikki/

www.instagram.com/nikkimoyesauthor/

www.goodreads.com/author/show/15606198.Nikki_Moyes

Free Short Story: THE HALFLING - The dragon Bronzrr dreams of becoming the next Story Keeper for his clan, but to do so he'll have to destroy the friendship he has with the little halfling outcast, Sapphia.

Grab your free ebook copy here:

https://nikkimoyes.com/index.php/newsletter/

Other books by Nikki Moyes

www.ingramcontent.com/pod-product-compliance
Lightning Source LLC
Chambersburg PA
CBHW070400120726
47909CB00008B/2933